A GENTLEMAN'S GIFT

A PRIDE AND PREJUDICE HOLIDAY VARIATION

CELIA NORMAN

DARCY

It was a beautiful autumn day, but Fitzwilliam Darcy was hard pressed to notice the light chill of the breeze and the warmth of the sunlight that poured through the slowly changing leaves on the branches above his head.

Quite the opposite. He would have preferred to be anywhere else in the world at that moment.

He could have been riding his horse over the rolling hills of Pemberley's estate, or visiting his tenant farmers, or speaking to the gamekeeper about the new pheasants that had just arrived... But, much to his great disdain, he strode through Hyde Park in the middle of busy London.

He was here at his aunt's insistence, and not even he could deny Lady Catherine de Bourgh what she demanded.

He had never paid any attention to the London season, but Georgiana was coming to an age where such things did, indeed, matter. And there was every indication that his aunt would expect for a prudent match to be made when that time came. If such a thing was to be achieved, Darcy would have to familiarize himself with the process, and at least go through the motions of knowing what to expect. His time in London had only just begun, and already he was tired of it.

He hated the long hours of socializing and the pointless tea parties and banquets. They always seemed to drag on with no real point or progress. There had to be something more substantial than dances, carriage rides, and operas.

There was something strangely off-putting about seeing every eligible young lady of a certain society on parade in their finery. How could he even think to subject Georgiana to such a thing? She would love it, no doubt. Expensive gowns, all of the music and attention—she would be in heaven.

Even though their own family was not in a position to gain much attention, Lady Catherine would see that the proper connections and introductions were made. Georgiana could do worse than a lord for a husband.

If he had his own way, he would be far from London and the buzz of the social scene—and dear Georgiana would have to content herself with meeting a prospective husband in some other manner.

Fitzwilliam Darcy understood very well that these events doubled as opportunities for well-bred young ladies to be introduced to well-moneyed gentlemen, but unlike every other gentleman present at the dinners, dances, operas, and other trifles he attended, he was *not* in want of a wife.

There was a time that he had felt such stirrings, but he had ruined all of that with his arrogant tongue and a disastrous proposal that he wished more than anything that he could take back.

He knew now that he deserved every moment of Elizabeth Bennet's scorn and even her wrath… It did not help matters that the memory of her heated refusal of his most ill-phrased offer haunted his every step.

If he could find some way to make amends, he would take it. If only to assuage his tempestuous conscience.

His mind clouded with frustration and annoyance directed entirely at himself, Fitzwilliam Darcy turned a quick corner and encountered a woman.

In essence it was more than an encounter; for the collision was entirely preventable, and he nearly knocked the young lady off her feet.

His neck heated with embarrassment as he tried to regain his bearings and reached out to help the woman he had so unceremoniously collided with.

"I must apologize," he choked out. "That was completely foolish of me. I was… I was not watching where I was going, and the hedgerow blocked my view—I am not familiar with this park—"

"Oh, dear!" another voice exclaimed and Darcy immediately felt his embarrassment grow as he realized that there had been a witness to his inattention.

"It's nothing, really. I'm fine," the woman replied. Her voice was filled with a hint of clear amusement at his flustered state.

He lifted his gaze, finally, to look at her. She wore a plain muslin dress better suited to a walk in the country than a turn about Hyde Park in the middle of the Season. Her dark eyes sparkled with laughter, fine eyes that he recognized all too well.

Realization dawned in those honeyed depths as quickly as it swept over him.

"Miss Bennet," he spluttered.

Her mouth fell open, and the faint pink in her cheeks darkened. "Mr. Darcy, whatever are you—"

"Oh, Mr. Darcy!" the other woman exclaimed.

Darcy bowed shortly as he recognized the other woman as Elizabeth Bennet's aunt, Mrs. Gardiner.

Their brief visit to Pemberley last August had left an indelible impression upon him and Mr. Gardiner had proved to be a diverting fishing partner.

"I must apologize," he said stiffly, embarrassed not only at how he had come upon them, but also by the fact that he had been distracted by thoughts of the very woman who now stood before him with a strange expression upon her face and an undeniable twinkle in her eye not unlike the one that had first drawn his attention.

"Mr. Darcy," Elizabeth said finally. "I did not expect to see you in London. Though, given the time of year, I suppose that I should not be surprised."

"Indeed," he said. "It is not my usual habit to be in London, but I am here on business—"

"Business, I did not realized that was what gentlemen referred to the Season as… Perhaps that is for the best. Please, do not let us keep you from your *business*," Elizabeth said stiffly.

It was with a pang of regret that Darcy realized that any affinity that might have been built since their meeting at Pemberley last summer had been well and truly forgotten.

It was, once more, entirely his fault for not pursuing the feelings that he struggled so mightily against.

Elizabeth curtseyed quickly and turned to walk away, but mrs. Gardiner paused and Darcy noted the pained glance she cast in her niece's direction.

"Lizzy, do wait," Mrs. Gardiner said before turning her attention to him. "Mr. Darcy, as you are in London, it would be remiss of me not to invite you to tea. Perhaps you would do us the honor of coming to our house in Gracechurch Street. I know my husband would be very glad to see you—he talks of nothing but the fine brown trout he caught in Pemberley's lake last summer."

Mr. Darcy smiled at the unexpected invitation, and noted how Elizabeth's expression twisted at the thought of his coming to tea, but the change was brief. Her smile, however, seemed strained and that familiar pang of regret returned with violent force.

He needed to speak with her. He had to apologize. He did not know how to find the words to make her understand what it was he had meant to do... but he would have to try.

Perhaps this would be the perfect opportunity to do so.

"I would be delighted to attend," he said warmly.

Mrs. Gardiner smiled, but almost relieved that he had agreed. "Wonderful," she replied. "We shall expect you in two days' time."

"I shall be looking forward to it." He bowed again as the women moved away down the path, but he caught Elizabeth Bennet's resentful glare as they turned a corner to walk by the carefully cultivated rose gardens.

He breathed a sigh of relief and ran a hand through his unruly dark hair. He had been invited to entirely too many teas and luncheons during his time in London, but this invitation was different.

It would be a welcome distraction from the confusion of haughty indifference and hungry stares of the ladies who attended such events. However, he would have to find a way to turn Elizabeth Bennet's dark looks into something kinder.

Indifference was entirely preferable to bitterness, and he would do whatever it took to make that so.

He had two days to plan his approach. And two days to repair what he had so negligently broken through his own inaction. For the fourth time that day he cursed his hesitation and his petty pride. He had lamented over his position more times than he cared to admit, and the more time passed, the more he knew that his thoughts and wishes did bend the same way as they had so many months ago.

There was no one else he would rather share his life with, but he had much to atone for, and Elizabeth Bennet had to decide if she felt the same...

Could there be anything he could do, or say, that would turn her thoughts back to the fondness she had for him last summer? Was such a thing even possible? Or had too much time, and too much bitterness, fallen between them?

ELIZABETH

"Lizzy, *do* slow down," Mrs. Gardiner puffed as she struggled to keep pace with her niece. But Elizabeth could not slow her steps, nor the furious beating of her heart.

How dare he?

He had very nearly knocked her to the ground with his carelessness!

How shocking to know that nothing had changed in the months since they had last spoken.

But something had changed. She had hoped, perhaps without cause, that their meeting would renew something between them. That she had changed somehow—or that he had... But nothing had happened.

She had spent the last months thinking of him only with bitterness and anger as days turned into weeks and the seasons changed around her. There had been a faint hope as Christmas had drawn close that the Bingley's would return to Netherfield Park, but the great house had remained conspicuously dark, and though

Jane had done her best to hide her disappointment, Elizabeth had noticed immediately. It was hard to watch her sweetest sister fall prey to melancholy over such a thing, but a broken heart was difficult to mend, and without the closure of knowing why she had been abandoned in such a way— Impossible.

"I do apologize," Elizabeth said with a sigh. "I am distracted…"

"So I can see," Mrs. Gardiner said with a sly smile as Elizabeth slowed her pace so that her aunt could regain her breath. "Would it have anything to do with seeing Mr. Fitzwilliam Darcy here in London?"

Elizabeth could not run from the blush that crept up her cheeks. "No, indeed," she lied quietly. Mrs. Gardiner did not look convinced, but thankfully she did not remark upon it.

"Then you do not mind that I have invited the gentleman to tea? Your uncle will be very pleased to see him."

"I am sure it will be a lovely engagement," Elizabeth said, but she was already thinking of how she could conspire to be out of the house before he arrived. Perhaps she could convince her aunt to send her on some errand or other. Or she could pretend to wish to go to the shops to purchase something for her sisters. She had promised Kitty some new ribbons, and Mary had requested a new quill for writing her musical compositions. These items were easily obtained in Meryton, of course, but somehow the items that came from London were more special and desired than the ones that were readily available.

"Do you think he prefers date scones? Would he take issue with sugared almonds? Perhaps lemon tarts instead…" Mrs. Gardiner wondered aloud.

"I do not think about him at all," Elizabeth blurted out. Mrs. Gardiner smiled and she threaded her arm through Elizabeth's as they crossed the park.

"Oh, my dear," she said. "I believe you have given *entirely* too much thought to a certain gentleman from Derbyshire since last we saw him," Mrs. Gardiner observed merrily.

Elizabeth's eyes widened, but she could not think of the

proper words to reply. She could not very well argue with her aunt, for Mrs. Gardiner was, of course, correct in her assumption.

"I—"

"You do not need to explain anything to me, Lizzy. The gentleman is everything your mother could wish for a suitor to be. He is in possession of a fine estate which you have seen for yourself, a goodly income, a handsome face…"

"Indeed," Elizabeth agreed bitterly.

"And is this not enough for you?" Mrs. Gardiner asked. "It was very clear to me when we visited Pemberley that the gentleman has some affection for you. Perhaps more than a little."

"It is a pity he cannot show it properly," Elizabeth snapped. Mrs. Gardiner pressed her lips together and Elizabeth immediately regretted her outburst. It was not her aunt's fault that the gentleman had ruined their walk. Could she bring herself to explain what had happened between them? She had not told a soul of his terrible proposal, not even Jane.

It was a secret that sat upon her heart like a canker on a rose and no amount of wishing would make it go away.

"Lizzy," Mrs. Gardiner said gently. "If there is something preventing you from allowing yourself to feel any affection for this gentleman, perhaps you should examine why that might be…"

"It is simple," Elizabeth blurted out. The ducks nearby, startled by her sudden exclamation, quacked in annoyance and waddled away from the footpath.

Mrs. Gardiner laughed at their antics, and Elizabeth felt some of her anger soften just a little. She sighed heavily. "I thought it was simple," she admitted quietly.

"Perhaps you will be able to tell me if we walk on a little farther," Mrs. Gardiner said encouragingly.

Elizabeth walked beside her aunt in silence for some minutes, but all at once, everything came pouring out. How he had insulted her upon their first meeting, how rude and arrogant he had been at Netherfield Park, his terrible proposal—and his conspiracy to drive Jane and Mr. Bingley apart.

It was that which she could not forgive.

More than a year had passed since she had discovered his part in Jane's cruel heartbreak. If he had bound that wound with an apology, and turned his friend once more to Hertfordshire, Elizabeth could have put aside her hurt and everything else—but Mr. Bingley had not appeared at Netherfield Park, and no letters had arrived at Longbourn for Jane… Not even so much as a reply to her desperate requests for some sign of affection from Caroline Bingley and Louisa Hurst.

"How could I forgive him for such things?" Elizabeth asked desperately. "No matter what my mother might say, a fine estate and ten thousand a year does *not* make a gentleman worthy of affection!"

"No, indeed," Mrs. Gardiner said softly. She had listened to all that her niece had to say with no more than a sympathetic smile upon her face. "May I offer some advice?" she asked.

"Yes, please," Elizabeth said miserably. "I am at a loss for words—and now he is to come to tea and I must confess I am dreading the arrival of that day! Please say that you will send me on any errand. Any tiny task that I might be out of sight and away from the house when he comes!"

Mrs. Gardiner patted her hand. "My poor girl," she said. "If I had known, I would have taken a very different approach. I merely hoped to rekindle some of those emotions I observed between you that day at Pemberley."

"It was so long ago," Elizabeth said. "I have half-forgotten what it felt like to see him again."

"Quite different from how you felt today," Mrs. Gardiner observed.

"Indeed," Elizabeth agreed with a small laugh.

"Have you considered, perhaps, asking the gentleman if he

had any intention of writing these wrongs he has done against you?"

Elizabeth's eyes widened, but her steps did not falter. "Ask him?"

"Quite so," Mrs. Gardiner said thoughtfully. "If you would but *ask* him to speak to Mr. Bingley on Jane's behalf—"

"But— I could do no such thing!" Elizabeth exclaimed. "I could not!"

"And why not? Jane does not know the part that the gentleman played in Mr. Bingley's absence from Netherfield Park. It would do no more harm than has already been done. If he agrees, then all may be well for Jane. And if he refuses—"

"Then all my ill will is justified," Elizabeth finished her aunt's sentence.

Mrs. Gardiner sighed. "It would seem so." They walked in silence for a time, and Elizabeth turned her aunt's words over in her mind and tried to decide how she had felt to see him again.

Her emotions were as confused as her thoughts… She had been embarrassed, angry, and, at the same time, breathless when his dark eyes met hers.

Her aunt was correct about many things. Elizabeth *had* spent too much time thinking about him. About how different he had been at Pemberley to the disagreeable gentleman she had known in Hertfordshire. But all of that consideration and change meant nothing when no action had followed their meeting. He had proven nothing by his actions.

Nothing.

Of that, Elizabeth could be certain.

"Will you consider it?" Mrs. Gardiner asked. Her aunt's voice broke through the fog of Elizabeth's thoughts, and she nodded slowly.

"I suppose there is no other option. If Mr. Darcy has ever held me in any regard, I should think he would consider my request.

He has said in the past that his good opinion, once lost, could never be regained…"

"Then you have nothing to lose," Mrs. Gardiner said firmly.

"That is very true," Elizabeth agreed with some surprise.

She smiled for the first time and tucked her arm into the crook of her aunt's elbow. "Let him come to tea, and I shall confront him with my request."

"Perhaps after your uncle has enjoyed a tart or two," Mrs. Gardiner said. "I cannot abide a guest leaving only moments after their arrival."

"Indeed, I promise to hold my tongue until after the cakes are served," Elizabeth laughed.

Mrs. Gardiner patted Elizabeth's hand and smiled. "Your uncle will be most grateful."

3

DARCY

For all of the social events he had prepared himself for during his time in London, Fitzwilliam Darcy had not been nervous about any of them for none of those events had meant anything. But this, a simple invitation to tea at the house of a tradesman, actually meant something. Mr. Gardiner was a pleasant sort of man, and Darcy had enjoyed his company at Pemberley.

But it was not just the invitation that gave him pause, it was the fact that he would have to face Elizabeth Bennet and her furious looks.

In the year that had passed since seeing her at Pemberley, his thoughts had often strayed to wondering about what she was doing. He tortured himself with wondering if she was happy in Hertfordshire—and whether or not she had accepted a proposal from one of the militia officers, or a local gentleman. The son of Meryton's only lawyer, perhaps...

But if he could judge from the confused mixture of surprise, embarrassment, and anger in her expression... it would seem that she had not spent that time in positive reflection upon him.

The flare of hope that she had not accepted any proposals also threatened to drive him mad. He had agonized over what might have happened to turn her thoughts against him. He still regretted every word of his terrible proposal—though they had seemed correct and true at the time, he knew that he had taken a fundamentally flawed approach and damaged whatever good grace he might have hoped to cultivate with her. He had hoped to ease any tension with his intervention on Mr. Wickham's scandalous betrayal. But that had only seemed to pause the tension between them, and not correct it entirely.

"Damn," he whispered as he fumbled with his neckcloth.

He should not have been this clumsy.

"Can I help you with that, sir?" his valet said quickly and Darcy sighed with resignation as he allowed the man to tie the neckcloth and help him into his jacket.

"I shall return at four," he said briskly as the valet handed him his pocket watch.

"Of course, sir. There is a reception at Lady Montgomery's this evening, and an invitation arrived for a boating party—"

A boating party? He could think of nothing more tedious and unappealing than being trapped on the Thames with a group of people he could not bring himself to speak to.

"Cancel them all," Darcy snapped.

He was tired of all of it.

Every single superficial event, every simpering conversation conducted in his presence or aimed in his direction.

Seeing Elizabeth Bennet had reminded him, very sharply and unexpectedly, that he was not sampling the London season in search of a wife—he had already found the companion of his heart and hearth… But she did not want him.

"I shall be returning to Derbyshire at the end of the week. See to the arrangements."

"Of course, sir," the man replied and Darcy gave his reflection another cursory glance before he walked from the room at a brisk pace. His mind was full of only one thing—Elizabeth

Bennet's fine eyes. He had seen them in many states over the course of a few months, but he liked them best when they sparked with merriment, even if it was at his own expense.

She had a sharp wit, and would leap upon any argument… He liked her enthusiasm for truth, and enjoyed her challenges.

But the way she had looked at him in Hyde Park—he did not want to see that sort of clouded anger in those honeyed eyes ever again. He had a mind to set it right. Surely, there was something he could do.

The carriage the valet had ordered for him waited at the curb, but Darcy was far too agitated to sit. He strode through the foyer with determined steps and the valet opened the front door for him. As he descended toward the cobbled street, the driver jumped down from his seat to open the carriage door, but Darcy waved him away.

"I shant require the carriage," he said briskly. "Which way to Gracechurch Street?" he asked. The driver, flustered at having his schedule knocked asunder, stared at him.

"Are you certain, sir?" he asked. "It is almost two miles—"

"I am very certain, indeed," Darcy replied testily. He knew it would be a long walk, but he needed to clear his head, lest he embarrass himself or speak too passionately when confronted with the object of his most ardent admiration. For he did still feel it—those confusing emotions he could not extinguish. In fact, unlike Elizabeth, it seemed that his admiration for her had only increased as time passed. He wondered what she would say if he told her that in a moment of failed judgement.

The driver sighed heavily and gestured in a vague direction. "Take the next left to St. Martin in the Fields, and walk on to the Strand, and then bear right to Fleet Street and St. Paul's Cathedral…"

"I shall ask for directions as I approach the Cathedral," he said.

"Very good, sir," the driver said with a shrug. He climbed back up into his seat and snapped his reins across the back of the horse who broke into a brisk trot as the carriage pulled away from the curb.

The valet's expression was confused, but Darcy did not feel the need to explain. "Are you quite sure—" the man called out.

"Quite," he replied shortly. "I shall return before nightfall."

"As you say, Sir."

Without backward glance Darcy set off in the direction the driver had indicated. He checked his pocketwatch and allowed himself a hint of hope that he would not be late.

It would not take him long to walk to Gracechurch Street, of that he was certain.

All he could hope was that Miss Elizabeth Bennet would be in the right frame of mind to speak with him. If she refused to see him, it would all be for naught.

4

ELIZABETH

Elizabeth Bennet's fingers fumbled with the dusky orange ribbons at the shoulder of the ivory muslin dress she had chosen. The color of the ribbons mimicked the color of the leaves on the oak tree across the street from her aunt and uncle's house and reminded her of the approach of autumn and the nearness of her favorite time of year.

The reflection in the mirror was of a young woman who was fresh and rosy-cheeked. The dark orange ribbon looked well in her dark curls, and against her pale skin, but Elizabeth had felt dissatisfied with almost everything that day.

"You should not be so worried," she muttered. "It is only tea… not a luncheon, not supper."

Perhaps in the two days since their untimely collision in Hyde Park he might have changed his mind about his attendance. Perhaps it would be beneath him to come to this side of town and he had decided to send a boy bearing a note containing his regrets, instead.

It would only be proper for him to refuse. He had accepted Mrs. Gardiner's invitation out of politeness, but surely, reason would have prevailed and he would have seen the error of his ways…

Perhaps it was not too late for her to find some reason to venture into the city and avoid the event altogether…

"Lizzy, are you ready?"

Too late.

Mrs. Gardiner's face appeared in the doorway and Elizabeth sighed heavily. "I believe so."

"You look lovely," Mrs. Gardiner said with a smile.

Elizabeth smiled thinly but did not reply.

She did not *want* to look lovely, and, most of all, she dreaded having to look upon Mr. Darcy while she drank her tea.

"Come along, now," Mrs. Gardiner said briskly. "Mr. Darcy will arrive shortly."

Elizabeth followed her aunt down the stairs to the parlor that had been set with the Gardiner's finest china. Plates of lemon cakes, sugared almond tarts, scones dotted with fat currants, and a small bowl of bright raspberry preserve had been set out and Elizabeth's stomach growled just a little in protest.

She had been determined not to enjoy this engagement, but the addition of some of her favorite pastries would make that very difficult.

"I had hoped the almond tarts would put a smile upon your face," Mrs. Gardiner murmured as they entered the room.

"Mrs. Archer has outdone herself."

"Indeed," Mrs. Gardiner agreed. "It is not often that we have such distinguished guests for tea, I shall have to mention it personally when Mr. Darcy has gone."

Elizabeth nodded and took her seat near the window. She had not intended to sit where she could watch for Mr. Darcy's arrival, but somehow it had happened and she felt very self-conscious as her aunt noticed and smiled briefly.

As it had been when they were children, nothing escaped Mrs. Gardiner's watchful eye.

"I shall ring for the tea to be brought up when Mr. Darcy arrives," her aunt said briskly. "Now, where has Mr. Gardiner gone…" she muttered. "I shall have to go and find him, that man has a way of forgetting the most mundane engagements— Lizzy, I shall return in a moment, if you would wait here and welcome Mr. Darcy when he arrives?"

Elizabeth's stomach tightened, but she nodded briefly. "Of course," she replied.

In truth, Elizabeth would rather have done *anything* else, and her aunt's request had interrupted her desperate last minute plans to escape the parlor entirely.

What would she say to him when he arrived? Could she bring herself to welcome him calmly to the Gardiner's home and ring for tea? Surely, that would be enough. It would not take long for her aunt to locate her missing husband… surely. If the moment dragged on too long, she could abandon him in the parlor and go in search of them.

Simple.

The bell at the Gardiner's front door rang sharply and Elizabeth looked out the window in a panic. Already? But there was no carriage waiting at the curb.

She knotted her fingers in her lap as she saw a tall gentleman in a dark coat standing upon the front step. Elizabeth took a deep breath and hoped for calm, but it was not to be found. Mr. Gardiner's valet opened the door, and she could hear the low sound of their voices in the foyer.

He spoke to the gentleman on the stairs, and then the telltale sound of boots stepping over the threshold and onto the polished hardwood floors of the foyer reached her and all semblance of calm fled.

Elizabeth leapt out of her seat and walked quickly across the room to ring the bell for tea. That would provide a welcome distraction from having to speak to Mr. Darcy.

That morning, and while she was dressing, Elizabeth had

decided that she would confront him with her request. It would be a simple enough task to say the words that she had planned. She had rehearsed them in the mirror while she secured the orange ribbon around her dark curls.

"You must entreat Mr. Bingley to reconsider his decision to quit Netherfield Park..."

"Mr. Fitzwilliam Darcy," the valet intoned from the doorway. Elizabeth pulled the cord to ring for tea a little too firmly and she grimaced as she imagined the force at which that particular bell must have rung in the servery.

She smoothed down her skirts and folded her hands at her waist as Mr. Darcy entered the room. She smiled and curtsied briefly in response to his stiff bow.

"Thank you Mr. Martin," she said briskly. "Do you know where my uncle has gone?"

Mr. Malcolm appeared puzzled for a moment. "He is in his study with Mr. Carter, I believe," he said.

Elizabeth blinked in surprise. She had not known that anyone had come to call before Mr. Darcy arrived. How could he have scheduled a meeting on the same day as this—

It did not matter.

Elizabeth thanked him again and the valet nodded and disappeared into the hallway. Mr. Carter was one of her uncle's dear friends, and there was no doubt in Elizabeth's mind that the man would occupy not only her uncle's time, but her aunt's as well.

She could not help but think that her aunt had planned this little... *delay* on purpose.

Mr. Darcy stood in the doorway awkwardly and Elizabeth bit her lip as she tried to think of what to do. One thing was certain, she could not leave him standing there forever.

"Will you sit down," Elizabeth said as she returned to her seat by the window.

"You are very kind," Mr. Darcy replied quietly as he searched for an appropriate spot. Not too near where she sat, nor too far away.

To any casual observer, the scene must have looked utterly ridiculous. Her, seated near the window, as far away from the table set with tea time pastries as possible, and the gentleman positioned somewhat stiffly on a chair that was most certainly too small for his long frame.

The couch would have been a more appropriate seat, but that would have been too close…

How could her aunt leave her alone in this manner?

A *purposeful betrayal.*

Mr. Darcy cleared his throat and Elizabeth glanced in his direction, but only briefly.

"I trust your family is well," he said.

"Yes, I thank you. Very well," she replied politely.

"And your sister, Lydia?"

Elizabeth paused. He had every right to ask after Lydia's happiness, it had been because of him that she, and all of them, had been saved from ruin. She shifted in her seat and forced herself to smile. "Quite well," she said. "She is expecting her third child."

Mr. Darcy's answering nod was slow and measured, and she wondered if his thoughts ever strayed to the rogue she was now forced to call 'brother.' Did he feel any regrets for lending his assistance to the Bennet family in their hour of dire need?

He was sitting so near, she could just… ask him.

"Mr. Darcy, I have not had occasion to ask this of you in the past," she began.

His dark gaze met hers and Elizabeth swallowed thickly. He was still so handsome, and he still looked at her as though she were the most important person in the whole of London—no, not just London—the whole world.

The realization stunned her, but only for a moment before she regained her courage.

"You did not have to intervene… That is to say, it was not your responsibility—"

But her words faltered and Elizabeth looked down at her hands to escape the warmth of his gaze.

"I am afraid that I must argue with you, Miss Bennet," he said gently. "It was entirely my responsibility to see that Mr. Wickham's past treachery did not become—"

He paused for a moment and seemed to gather his thoughts. Elizabeth waited patiently, uneasy with the fact that she had caught him off guard. "The situation that I feared would befall my own sister—one that I barely saved her from. I could not permit it to happen to anyone else. I should have done more to warn you of his inclinations before he set his sights upon Lydia."

Elizabeth sighed. "Lydia is not a wise girl," she said ruefully.

"I would wager that none of us is wise at that age," Mr. Darcy said kindly. "I am glad to hear that she is well and happy."

"Happy may not be the most accurate word," Elizabeth said with a rueful smile, "but she is still very pleased to be the only one of her sisters who is married. Did you know that she named her first son after you?"

"I received a card at Pemberley," he said with a smile.

Elizabeth scolded herself for mentioning that Lydia was still the only one of them that had found herself a husband.

Despite the fact that it was a position which had been acquired in a most disagreeable manner, it had not stopped Lydia from elevating herself above her elder sisters with great delight.

"What I did not say," he continued after a moment, "what I *could* not say, was that I could not let it happen to anyone, but especially not your beloved sister. I have labored long over my inability to speak about the truth of Mr. Wickham's treachery. I had hoped—I still hope—that he is a changed man. What he did to my family was done out of spite and cruelty. It was nothing more than revenge against myself and my father for a slight that was not meant as he saw it. He did not love Georgiana, and I could not allow you to experience that same pain."

"Indeed," Elizabeth agreed. "He did you a great disservice…" and then her voice faded as she realized what he had said.

He had done all of it for her.

She had planned to be so very strong. She had planned to confront him for his cruelty to Jane—but all of the words she had hoped to say had melted away.

No.

She must say them.

"But you have done a greater disservice to another of my dear sisters," she said firmly.

Mr. Darcy's eyes widened and Elizabeth felt a small stab of victory at having surprised him once more.

"Jane," she said. "You told me in your letter of how you convinced Mr. Bingley that Jane had no affection for him. Quite proudly, in fact."

Elizabeth could feel the rage bubbling up inside her and she could not stop her angry words.

"I know my sister, and I know the depth of her affection for Mr. Bingley—you cannot comprehend the sorrow and confusion she felt when we received word that he had left Netherfield Park. But it was Miss Bingley's insistence that they would never return, and their refusal to even *see* Jane when she was here in London— it was *that* which truly broke her heart."

Elizabeth's eyes burned with unshed tears as she remembered Jane's pain and heartache. How she had withdrawn from the family, and refused to speak of it. Of how she had promised that she would be 'herself' once again… in time.

But that time had not come.

"It was unbearable to watch her suffer," she finished quietly. "It is unbearable how much she *still* suffers."

More than a year had passed, and another Christmas approached with Netherfield Park standing empty, and Jane had still not shown any sign of forgetting Mr. Bingley or the affection she held for him.

If Mr. Darcy only knew how many officers she had refused, how many young men had come to speak to their father and inquire after her hand…

But he knew nothing, and he had not cared.

He had been concerned only with himself and his own selfish pride.

Mr. Darcy looked down at his hands which gripped the edge of his hat tightly. "I…"

"I know what you will say," she said bitterly. "You will say that you did not realize she would be hurt. After all, how could she be hurt if she held so little affection for him?"

Mr. Darcy rose from his chair and strode across the room toward her. Elizabeth feared for a moment that she had said too much and angered him, but then she decided that she did not *care* if he was upset.

She straightened her shoulders and her fingers twisted in her lap.

"You are correct," he said as he seated himself on the couch beside her. He laid his hat upon the cushions between them and looked into her eyes. "I did not consider your sister's feelings. I thought only of my friend…"

Elizabeth lifted her chin and looked into his eyes.

"Miss Bennet… Elizabeth. I hope—" He looked down at his hand, clenched into a fist upon his knee, and then back up at her. "I hope that you can forgive me. That somehow you can find it in your heart to take my apology for whatever value it holds."

"A delayed apology, indeed," Elizabeth said quietly.

"What would you have me do?" he asked. "What would you ask of me to make this right?"

Elizabeth's frantic thoughts almost drowned out his words.

What would she ask of him?

What did she want?

She wanted to strike him. To shout at him.

But none of it would do her any good.

She stiffened as he reached out and took her hands in his, but Elizabeth could not pull her fingers away—nor did she want to.

"Tell me," he said softly. "Name it, and I will do as you ask."

Elizabeth bit her lip as her heart pounded in her chest and her thoughts tumbled like dry leaves.

What would she ask of him?

"I must ask you," Elizabeth said haltingly, "No. I must beg you to speak to Mr. Bingley. On behalf of my sister, but also—for yourself. You must tell him that you were misled in your thinking. You must tell him that you did not understand what you were asking of him. Bring him back to Hertfordshire." Her eyes searched his and she found herself almost lost within their dark depths.

His jaw tightened.

"I shall do as you ask," he said.

"And if you still have doubts, it will take only a few hours to know for certain if you were correct—and then you have lost nothing but time..." Elizabeth's words trailed away as he nodded.

"I shall do as you ask," he repeated.

"How do I know that you will?"

He smiled briefly. "You have my word… as a gentleman." He lowered his voice and leaned closer. "And my word, as a man who still ardently loves and admires you."

His lips were so close to hers, close enough that she could feel the warmth of his breath upon her cheek.

"A gentleman's word," Elizabeth said softly. "How can I trust such a thing when it is a gentleman's word that has changed so much—"

She could not finish her sentence, for Mr. Darcy closed the distance between them and pressed his lips to hers.

It was the briefest kiss.

Only a moment.

But her lips burned with the pressure of it and a sudden twist in her stomach that she could not explain.

Anger, embarrassment, and something like shame burrowed into her consciousness as she pulled away.

How dare he take such liberties—

"Lizzy? Lizzy, I am so sorry to have kept you waiting—has Mr. Darcy arrived? I do hope not..." Mrs. Gardiner's voice floated down the hallway and pierced through the fog that filled Elizabeth's mind.

Elizabeth pressed her hand to her lips as Mr. Darcy stood and moved toward the window.

Mr. and Mrs. Gardiner entered the room all smiles and jovial greetings with one of the maids, following close behind with the tea that Elizabeth had rung for.

It seemed like ages had passed since Mr. Darcy had arrived, and Elizabeth choked on her surprise as she watched the gentleman greet her aunt and uncle.

They settled themselves into chairs and Elizabeth had to force herself to take a breath and pretend that nothing was amiss.

Mrs. Gardiner poured tea, but though she knew that she should help, Elizabeth could only sit upon the couch and watch their interactions.

Mr. Darcy seemed fond of the biscuits with raspberry preserve, Elizabeth noted, but he did not seem overfond of tea. Perhaps he was partial to the Chinese blends that had begun to appear in the shops in Meryton... Or even coffee—

Ridiculous thoughts.

"Lizzy, are you quite well?" Mrs. Gardiner asked suddenly, and Elizabeth realized that she had been asked a question that she had not heard.

"I am... I do apologize, I— I believe I need some air," she said. She set down her tea and pushed herself to her feet. Mr. Darcy and Mr. Gardiner both fumbled with their cups to stand up with her.

"Lizzy—" her aunt said with concern, but Elizabeth was not listening, she was desperate to leave the room. She could not listen to them talking so nonchalantly while her heart and her mind were so at war.

"I shall return in a moment," she murmured. "Please, do not stop on my account."

She left the room as quickly as she was able, half-wondering whether her aunt would follow, or if she would be left to her own devices.

Elizabeth had only taken ten steps down the hallway on shaking legs when she felt a hand upon her elbow.

"Elizabeth."

That voice. The one she had heard so often in her dreams… The one she could admit now that she had desired to hear in her waking hours, too.

"Why have you followed me?" she asked breathlessly as she turned to look into the gentleman's eyes.

"To tell you again that I will heed your demands," he said.

"I will hold you to your promise," Elizabeth said. "A gentleman's word."

"Will you come back to tea?" he asked. His eyes burned with something that she could not define, but there was no denying that their brief interaction had awoken something inside her that she had almost forgotten.

Elizabeth shook her head. "I could not… I have letters to write. Please convey my apologies to my aunt. You may tell her that I am unwell. The warmth of the room—the stress of company… Any excuse you please."

"And will you say nothing to my admission," he choked out.

"Your admission?" Elizabeth smiled ruefully. "When you have done as you have promised—only then will I be able to trust anything that you might offer. No matter how clumsily that offer might be made."

The gentleman's lips pressed into a thin line, and he nodded briefly.

"I shall make your apologies," he said.

"Thank you," she whispered.

She ached to kiss him again, but could not bring herself to do so. Her aunt could emerge from the parlor at any moment, or her uncle. And she could not bear the possibility of scandal.

Without another word, Elizabeth walked toward the stairs and did not look back at the gentleman as he stood in the hallway. She could not imagine what he was thinking—all she knew was that her own mind was a cacophony of noise and confusion.

She knew what she wanted—at least, she thought she did—but whether she would be able to have it was another problem entirely.

What if he did not keep his promise? What if he did not bring Mr. Bingley back to Hertfordshire and Netherfield Park…

Elizabeth climbed the stairs as quickly as she could and stepped into her bedchamber and closed the door tightly behind her.

She leaned against it and let out a frustrated breath.

What if nothing happened?

She would be alone.

Jane would never accept any other proposal.

Could happiness truly exist for her? Or would she be caught forever in the maelstrom of confusion that threatened to overwhelm her.

Elizabeth paced the room and then sat upon her bed.

She would be returning to Hertfordshire in a matter of days—Mr. Darcy would have to prove himself a gentleman of his word, or lose her affection forever.

But with the memory of his kiss upon her lips and the heat of his hands still upon her skin, Elizabeth did not know if she could hold herself to such a threat…

5

DARCY

He watched Elizabeth climb the stairs, moving as quickly as she dared, and Darcy fought the urge to chase after her. He had dared too much in their conversation. Dared too much by kissing her.

She has abandoned you, Darcy, a voice in his mind whispered.

"Ah, Mr. Darcy! Will you return to the parlor? Or has something called you away?"

He turned to see a smiling Mr. Gardiner at the parlor doorway.

"No, no, indeed. I do apologize." He strode down the corridor with a smile upon his face and entered the parlor once more. "Miss Bennet has asked that I apologize on her behalf. She was… taken ill."

Mrs. Gardiner's eyes widened. "Ill?"

"She asked that you not worry about her," he said hastily. "It is only the warmth of the room— She will be herself soon enough. She promised as much."

Mrs. Gardiner did not seem convinced, but she did not argue and Darcy hoped that he had said enough so as not to arouse any suspicion.

He took a seat once more and accepted a fresh cup of tea. He was not partial to the traditional sort of tea served in London's parlors and made a mental note to ask his valet to order more chai from his contact in St. George's Square,

"You are in London for the Season, I take it?" Mr. Gardiner asked.

"I am," Darcy replied. "My sister, Georgiana, is to come up next summer. My aunt will be making her introduction and presentations, and I wished to be certain of what she would face in her time here."

"How fortunate to have such connections," Mrs. Gardiner said. "And what is your opinion of the London season?"

"It is entirely too dull for me, I daresay," Darcy admitted. "I have no stomach for frivolous entertainments and turns about the park."

"But that was precisely where we found him," Mrs. Gardiner said to her husband.

All at once Darcy wished that he could escape the parlor as well—he had made Elizabeth Bennet a promise, and he meant to keep it. If only to see her again.

But he could not run away from this invitation, so he was forced to smile and try desperately to think of a way to extricate himself from this situation as soon as possible.

But as the conversation began to ebb and flow, Darcy found himself relaxing.

Not having Elizabeth there to distract him with her glares and frowns meant that he was able to talk with the Gardiners with ease.

They were pleasant folk, and they had enough experience of the country and the city to be well-versed in many topics that Darcy found interesting.

Mr. Gardiner was particularly enamored of fishing, and Darcy could have talked for hours with the gentleman about his experiences and the places he hoped to travel to stoke his penchant for the sport.

"He would walk all the way to Balmoral if I would allow it," Mrs. Gardiner laughed. "But he *will* insist on wearing tartan and always returns to London smelling of wet wool and sneezing with a head cold."

"It is not as bad as she says," Mr. Gardiner huffed as he helped himself to another biscuit.

"Certainly not," Mrs. Gardiner said with a smile. "Sometimes he even returns with salted fish for the cook to throw away!"

Mr. Darcy chuckled along with Mr. Gardiner who seemed very good humored about his wife's loving judgement of his hobby.

Darcy had never thought about marriage for an extended period of time, except when it came to Elizabeth Bennet... Since his terrible proposal at Hunsford, marriage was all he could seem to think about.

Specifically, what a marriage to Miss Elizabeth Bennet might be like. What it might be like to call her his wife, and have her call him 'husband.'

But he could say nothing of that here, and when it came time for him to leave, he found that he was not entirely eager to do so.

It had been a diverting afternoon, marred only by Elizabeth's absence and the promise he had made beating in his mind with the steadiness of his pulse.

Mr. and Mrs. Gardiner promised that he was welcome at their home whenever he should like to visit and Darcy thanked them for their kind offer before he turned to descend the stairs and make his way back to his rented rooms.

He stood on the sidewalk and turned back to raise a hand in farewell, and as the front door closed on the Gardiner's smiling faces, Darcy looked up and saw another face in the window of the room above.

Elizabeth.

Pale and beautiful, her expression was haughty and curious at the same time. He smiled up at her, hopeful that she had softened toward him, but her face disappeared from the window, replaced by a white curtain that hid her from view.

Darcy shook his head and chuckled to himself as he set off along the road. He had made a promise, and he would see it carried out.

But it was impossible to forget the feeling of Elizabeth's lips upon his. He had dared too much, that was true, but she had not rebuked him, and perhaps that was enough.

He rubbed his fingers over his mouth and smiled as he remembered the spark of desire in her eyes when she had looked at him. He would hold that thought in his mind for the rest of his days. He only hoped that it could be the beginning of something that he never knew he had longed for. But that was now his responsibility.

He could only hope that his reward would be as sweet as the memory he now carried with him.

6

DARCY

Alone in his chamber at the Middlemarch Club, Fitzwilliam Darcy realized that he would have to approach his friend with careful consideration. He recalled with a grimace how he had campaigned for Charles to leave Hertfordshire and forget his misguided infatuation with Jane Bennet.

He shook his head at his own misguided pride. Elizabeth had been correct, he *had* been cruel.

He smiled as the image of her determined face entered his mind.

She was exactly as he remembered her from Hertfordshire, and Hunsford—she was strong-willed and in possession of a sharp wit... But it was her care for her sisters that gave him the most pause. That she would put her elder sister's heart and happiness before her own was humbling.

It did not escape his notice that she held him personally responsible for the pain that Jane had suffered after Mr. Bingley's departure from Netherfield Park.

He had caused that pain willingly.

Thankfully, Charles had agreed to meet him at the Club for

supper, and he had precious little time to consider what he would say to convince his friend to return to Hertfordshire. He knew that despite Caroline and Louisa's insistence, Charles had not yet released his claim to the estate at Netherfield Park. Perhaps that could be where he could begin his discussion.

"What are you saying, Darcy?" Charles Bingley sat back in his chair and stared incredulously at his friend.

They had only just begun their supper. Rare steak, well peppered and exotically spiced—a specialty of the Club—had just arrived.

But Darcy ignored the steak and instead held his friend's surprised gaze without looking away as the steaks were set in front of them. "Netherfield Park," he repeated. "Do you think of it often?"

Charles looked down at his steak and reached for his knife. "I do," he said. "More often than I should like. Caroline tells me that I am foolish to continue to keep it, but—"

"But you cannot stop thinking about it," Darcy pressed.

Charles nodded, but Darcy could see that his friend had more to say. Though it was not fit for their conversation here. However, Darcy would not be deterred by such things.

"Perhaps I might have been too hasty to add my agreement to your sisters' demands to leave the countryside," he said.

Charles set down his knife and folded his hands upon the table. "I will not ask you again, William. Speak plainly, you are making my head ache and I have been thinking of this steak for the last week."

Darcy chuckled as his friend's candor. "I do not mean to put you off your food," he said.

"So what reason would you have for speaking of Hertford-shire?" Charles asked. "At our last meeting you would hear of nothing to do with Netherfield Park. Even Caroline could not match your bitterness for that place, and that is no mean feat."

Now it was Darcy's turn to grit his teeth and set down his knife. "I confess— I may have been overhasty in my..."

"Your anger? Your perseverance in convincing me that there was nothing for me in Hertfordshire—"

"I was wrong," Darcy interrupted him quietly.

Silence descended between them and the laughter from the other patrons seemed too loud as Charles stared at him.

"I beg your pardon?" he said.

"I was wrong," Darcy repeated.

"I daresay, I do not believe I have ever heard you utter those words," Charles said incredulously. "Will you explain?"

Darcy knew that there was no sense in avoiding the obvious. "I cannot speak of this in any other way."

"Well, out with it, man."

"It has to do with your affection for Miss Jane Bennet," Darcy said bluntly.

Charles looked down at his plate and sighed heavily. "What of it? You were opposed to my interest in her. As were Caroline and Louisa. I was right to listen to you and save myself from heartache..."

"I was wrong," Darcy admitted.

Apologies were difficult, and it seemed as though he had been overdue on several of them.

Charles sat forward in his chair. "I beg your pardon?" His friend's voice was quiet, and Darcy could not help the feeling of regret that stole over him, but he had to charge ahead.

This apology was the lynchpin to securing the heart of the woman to whom all of his thoughts and wishes turned.

"I was mistaken, Charles. And I must apologize for it."

He *was* sincere.

Decidedly.

And the flood of relief that accompanied those words only

served to solidify those feelings. He had been wrong to say such things when he, himself, was in the process of denying his own feelings towards Elizabeth Bennet. Perhaps he had used his feeling of betrayal at the wayward nature of his own heart as a weapon against his friend. Another failing to add to the growing list.

Charles appeared flabbergasted by this pronouncement. "Mistaken— But, Darcy, I…"

"I speak to you now, truly, and as your friend. It was wrong of me to give such an opinion. I was… I was mistrustful of the young lady's affections. I know not *why* I felt as I did, but I know that my feelings have changed. I know now that I have done you, and the young lady, a disservice."

"But Caroline… Louisa… They seemed so certain—"

Darcy sliced into his steak with a vicious stroke. "Jealousy, I would expect. Your sisters are not known for having the kindest of dispositions. Especially when their own interests are at stake. I imagine that Caroline has her own opinions as to whom you should marry."

Charles made a face and took a quick sip of his whiskey. "Indeed, she has been most insistent in her invitations to attend tea with one friend or another—all of whom seem to have a sister of marriageable age with a sizable income and some collection of accomplishments to recommend them."

Darcy allowed some silence to fall between them, but Charles appeared to be far away, and Darcy wondered what his friend was thinking.

"What if you were to return to Netherfield Park?" Darcy asked casually.

"Return to Netherfield Park— I suppose… I suppose I could. It would not be… Yes, I rather think it would be quite pleasant. Perhaps for Christmas. I should very much like to spend Christmas in my own country house. You always have Pemberley decorated so wonderfully, I have always been envious of it."

Darcy smiled. "I think a change of scenery would be a beneficial one. Georgiana has been alone too often in the last months, and I should think she would enjoy some time closer to London. Especially at Christmas."

"Yes," Charles mused. "Perhaps— Louisa and Caroline could not object to a Christmas in the countryside."

Darcy supposed that Caroline and Louisa could find several reasons to object to such a thing, but he did not say so. Instead, he smiled and picked up his whiskey glass.

He held it up in a toast and Charles did the same. "To Netherfield Park," he said.

"Indeed," Charles replied. "Netherfield Park and a country Christmas."

The crystal glasses clinked musically and Darcy congratulated himself on his conquest. As he had hoped, Charles had been easily convinced. Perhaps that meant he had not forgotten his affection for Jane Bennet, a possibility which would bode well for his own pursuits.

If they returned to Hertfordshire and Charles did not renew his suit, then it was not any fault of his. He could not control his friend's heart any more than he could control his own—but from the expression on Charles' face, it seemed that it would not take much to bring him back into Jane Bennet's arms.

***

With Charles' agreement, Darcy moved from the rooms he had rented at the club into the Bingleys' London home and all of his plans to return to Pemberley were put aside.

Preparations for their departure to Hertfordshire began at once, and while Caroline Bingley and Louisa Hurst complained bitterly at having their social calendars interrupted, the promise of Georgiana's arrival in London proved to be enough to distract them in the interim.

Darcy could not bring himself to push Charles to move any faster, but the promise he had made to Elizabeth burned in the back of his mind. Days turned into weeks, but it was the arrival of colder weather and the first December snowfall that made Darcy all the more eager to depart.

The day before they were set to depart, Louisa and Caroline seemed to have resigned themselves to their disappointment. While Caroline pouted, Louisa had begun to make plans for Christmas festivities at Netherfield Park.

Georgiana was due to arrive later that evening, and Caroline had been doing her utmost to obtain any scrap of gossip she could to prepare for her arrival.

Over supper, Darcy was subjected to question after question and his patience was wearing thin, though Caroline's interest seemed to only gather strength with each answer he gave her.

"Has dear Georgiana received any offers of marriage?" Caroline asked as the plates from the main course were swept away.

Darcy frowned at the forward nature of her question and shifted in his seat.

"There have been none that have come to me," he said. "I suspect that she will want to come to London for the season next year. I suppose that if there are any offers of marriage that come from her time in London, then I shall have to consider them most carefully."

"She is such a lovely and accomplished young woman," Caroline continued as though he had not replied. "It would be a shame to see her married to someone who did not deserve, or appreciate, such gifts."

"Indeed," Darcy agreed tersely. He did not know what Caroline's point was, and he did not care to find out. Surprisingly, in the last year, Caroline had somehow come to the realization that she could not win Darcy's affections, but she had not given up her interest in seeing her dear brother pay suit to Georgiana.

Darcy had several complaints about such a notion, foremost

among them being their difference in age… As much as he admired Charles as a friend, he would make a poor match for Georgiana.

Thankfully, each time Caroline had brought it up Charles had expressed no interest in such a match and Darcy was grateful for it.

But her brother's disinterest would not stop Caroline, the woman seemed to scheme even in her sleep.

"I do hope that there are no plans to renew our acquaintance with some of the residents of Meryton," Louisa sniffed. "Our departure was not well received, and I should not like to have any… uncomfortable invitations to tea."

Charles threw down his napkin. "What a *tragedy* that would be," he said stiffly.

Caroline turned surprised eyes to her brother and Darcy smothered his humor in his own napkin. Charles had clearly been thinking about the role his sisters had played in their abrupt departure from Hertfordshire.

"And what do you mean by that?" Caroline asked.

"Simply put, dear sister, if there are any *uncomfortable* situations in our future, they will be entirely the consequence of *your* own actions. Not mine. I, for one, am looking forward to the change of pace. London is too crowded and noisy, especially at this time of year. I long for the peace and tranquility of the countryside and the pleasant nature of the society."

"The society?" Caroline cried. "Pleasant?" She looked at Darcy in surprise. "Mr. Darcy, has my brother taken ill? Please tell me that you have not taken him to that horrid club to eat rare steak again? You know how it plagues his digestion!"

"Do not speak about me as though I were not in the room, Caroline," Mr. Bingley snapped.

Caroline and Louisa's shocked gasps at the sharpness of his tone were music to Darcy's ears. Charles' sisters had been looming over his life for far too long, and Darcy was pleased to see that his friend had finally seen them for who they truly were, even if it was only in a small way.

He just hoped that it would not be too late for his friend to find the happiness he sought... Just as he hoped that it would not be too late for himself.

Charles shifted in his chair and took a determined sip of his wine. "We will be staying at Netherfield Park through the New Year, so I suggest that you become resigned to the fact that we will welcome any and all visitors to our house. I will expect you to receive them graciously, and make them feel welcome."

Silence fell over the table as the servants returned to the dining room with the second course. Mr. Bingley replaced his napkin on his lap and picked up his utensils.

Caroline huffed into her wine and said nothing more.

Louisa was tight-lipped throughout the remainder of their supper and retired to bed before Georgiana arrived. Caroline seemed to forget her sullen anger soon after supper had been cleared away, and became her usual self as soon as Georgiana's carriage pulled up to the curb.

Though she was fatigued from her journey, Georgiana was excited for their early morning departure. Darcy watched from the corner of the room as his sister sat upon the couch with Caroline Bingley and asked questions about what she might expect from their journey and the countryside.

Charles had retired to his own chambers to prepare to leave, and Darcy could not blame him. He would have been even more angry at his sister if he could hear the answers to Georgiana's innocent questions.

Georgiana could be nothing but her sweet and lovely self, and she did not seem to notice the bitterness behind Caroline's words as she described Netherfield Park and Hertfordshire.

"And it is ever so dreadfully rainy and cold in the autumn, do you not agree, Darcy?" Caroline asked loudly. "I can only imagine the snow and ice that will descend upon it over Christmas!"

"How lovely," Georgiana exclaimed. "I do so love a fresh fall of snow. Pemberley is always so peaceful in the depths of winter." She wrinkled her nose. "Can you really prefer Christmas in London… The snow looks so ugly and grey after only a few days."

"You are a sweet girl, Georgiana," Caroline said with a sly smile, "but I daresay your brother has kept you too sheltered in your country home. You will feel quite comfortable in Hertfordshire."

Darcy could hear the scorn in Caroline's voice, and he rose from his chair and extended a hand to his sister. "I daresay she will," he said.

Georgiana smiled up at her brother and took his hand as she stood up from the couch. "I am certain that I will find no fault with it," she said brightly. "And I cannot think of a more wonderful time of year to spend in such a place."

"Indeed," Caroline mused.

Darcy could feel her eyes upon his back as he led Georgiana from the room, but he did not look back as he bid her goodnight.

"I am so looking forward to our time at Netherfield Park," Georgiana exclaimed as they walked through the corridor. "You have only mentioned it to me once before—and I cannot recall your own thoughts upon the place."

Darcy smiled and patted his sister's hand where it rested upon his elbow. "Netherfield Park is nothing to Pemberley, but I daresay that is not a fault. It is a beautiful estate, located in a lovely piece of the countryside. There are forests, and herds of wild deer… The hunting is excellent."

Georgiana giggled. "And what would I care about that?" she asked.

"Nothing, to be sure," Darcy said with a smile. "The society is… As tolerable as one might expect, but there are several country gentlemen with daughters your age, and I am certain that you will be able to find some accomplished young ladies with which to pass the time."

"Are any of them of an accomplishment that would interest you?" Georgiana asked carefully.

Darcy's eyebrow rose at her innocent question. "And what might you mean by that?"

"Oh, nothing," Georgiana teased him. "You have just spoken of Hertfordshire in such a way that I suspected there was more to your affection for it than excellent hunting. You were never much of a hunter, William."

She was not wrong, in either case, but he could not tell his sister anything about Miss Elizabeth Bennet. Though he did hope that once the dust had settled he could introduce the two young women. He felt certain that Elizabeth and Georgiana would make very agreeable friends.

"Perhaps it is the air," he said.

"Do we not have the same air in Pemberley?" Georgiana asked with a smile.

"Perhaps," Darcy replied, but he did not say anything else as they walked up the stairs to the second floor. Georgiana kissed his cheek and patted her brother upon the shoulder.

"Goodnight, William. Perhaps you will be able to show me precisely why you enjoy Hertfordshire once we arrive."

"Perhaps," he replied as the chamber door closed.

7

DARCY

In the morning, Mr. Bingley's sullen sisters climbed into the carriage with a smiling Georgiana following behind.

Though there was room in the carriage, Mr. Bingley and Mr. Darcy had chosen to ride alongside on horseback. They would make the journey much faster, and Darcy knew that his friend had chosen to ride for more reason than the speed of it.

"Has Mr. Weston been informed of our arrival?" Darcy asked unnecessarily. He knew that Charles had been prepared for their departure for weeks. Servants had gone on ahead to prepare the house, and he was certain that they would arrive at a welcoming house that was already decorated for the approaching Christmas season.

"Of course," Charles replied as he looked away from his younger sister's angry glare as the carriage door slammed shut.

"I fear you shall miss all of the important conversation," Darcy said meaningfully as he mounted his horse. "Such a pity."

"A great pity, indeed," Charles said with a small smile as he spurred his mount forward.

Darcy chuckled and followed his friend's lead. Without mishap, they would be in Meryton in a few hours. In any case, arriving earlier than the ladies would be preferable for all involved.

The approach of winter was evident in every mile of their journey, and Darcy knew it would not be long before the snow would be flying outside Netherfield Park's high windows.

Meryton was much as he remembered it, and the cobbled streets were filled with people. "Market day," Mr. Bingley said as they slowed their pace.

"It seems so," Darcy agreed. "Shall we ride on to Netherfield Park?"

"Yes—" But Charles was, very obviously, distracted.

"Charles?" His friend slid down from his saddle and threw the reins to Darcy who caught them awkwardly. "Where are you going?"

"I've just seen someone I would very much like to speak with," Charles said abruptly as he strode away.

Darcy watched in surprise as Charles approached a small knot of older gentleman and bowed deeply. It only took a moment before Darcy recognized the man Charles had chosen to speak to.

Mr. James Bennet III of Longbourn, Hertfordshire.

Miss Jane Bennet's father.

Darcy swallowed thickly as he watched the older gentleman excuse himself from his circle of friends and walk down the street with Charles Bingley.

Charles seemed to be wasting no time in the reaffirmation of his acquaintance with the Bennet family, and, indeed, it would follow that he would also renew his expressions of affection for Mr. Bennet's eldest daughter.

His heart beat strangely in his chest, and it began to make him think that he should have his own conversation with Mr. James Bennet.

F rom the expression upon Caroline Bingley's face, it was clear that she would never be happy at Netherfield Park. Her frown was firmly in place as their guests departed Netherfield Park's parlor.

The house smelled of rich pine and cinnamon spice, and Darcy could not help but feel comforted by the sheer amount of decoration that had been arranged around the house. Christmas was his favorite season, and he felt most at home in front of a roaring fire with snow falling outside the windows.

Snow had yet to make an appearance in Hertfordshire, but the sharpness of the wind and the dark gray clouds that loomed in the distance promised that would change soon enough.

"How many more guests must we receive for tea," Caroline grumbled.

"As I told you before we departed London, we shall receive as many guests as arrive on our doorstep," Mr. Bingley said firmly. "We have been absent from Hertfordshire for over a year. It is only natural that the inhabitants of the surrounding town will want to welcome us and see the wonderful decorations that the servants have put up for Christmas. It is tradition, Caroline, and one that I would be very happy to continue."

"As it seems," Caroline muttered.

"I think it is simply lovely," Georgiana exclaimed. "We have been at Netherfield Park only one week and there is already talk of an assembly to be held in our honor!"

"Surely not on account of us," Louisa said from a chair beneath the window. "It is almost Christmas; I would be shocked beyond all belief if there were not a regimental ball."

"Well, whatever the reason for it, we shall, of course, be attending," Charles said with a smile. Darcy had his suspicions that his friend had known this would be occurring, he may have even had a hand in its organization.

"*I* shall not be," Louisa announced. "It is too cold, and without any hint of snow. London is much warmer this time of year. We have made a mistake in coming here."

"It is no mistake," Charles laughed. "We are here for a change of scenery, Caroline. There is no place I would rather be."

His sister narrowed her eyes. "Indeed," she said. "I must say, Charles, there is one family I had expected to see upon our doorstep almost as soon as our carriage pulled into the courtyard."

Georgiana's eyes widened as Caroline Bingley's expression became sharp. Charles cleared his throat and adjusted his stance slightly.

"And who would that be?" Georgiana asked.

"Why, the Bennet's, of course," Caroline said.

Darcy did not like the saccharine sweetness of her tone, and even Georgiana seemed suspicious of it.

"Enough, Caroline," Mr. Bingley said.

"But that is the real reason we are here, Charles, is it not?" Louisa interjected. "How is it that those eager sisters and their vile mother neglected to darken these corridors?"

"Because they know better to invite themselves for tea," Caroline snapped. "It is just not done. It was unacceptable in London and—"

"I beg your pardon," Charles interrupted his sister. "London?"

Caroline's lips pressed together in a thin line and Louisa looked out the window at the frosty garden.

Georgiana's confusion was understandable, but Darcy could not bear to see Charles kept in the dark any longer.

"Miss Jane Bennet came to London, Charles," he blurted out. "After we left Netherfield Park, she came to take tea with your sisters. They did not receive her."

Aghast, Charles Bingley turned his eyes to Caroline who met his surprised stare boldly.

"Is this true?" he asked.

"It is," Caroline replied coldly. "Louisa and I made our position known when we left Netherfield Park. The fact that she attempted to continue our acquaintance once we had arrived in London is simply unconscionable."

Charles stood and glared down at his sister.

Darcy could not recall a time when he had ever seen his friend so angered.

"Mr. Darcy knew that we did not see her in London," Caroline said desperately. "It was *he* who encouraged us to ignore her letters."

"She wrote you letters and you did not answer them?" Charles' voice was quiet, but the anger in his tone was unmistakable.

"Caroline?"

She flinched as her brother's voice echoed in the room. "We did not," she whispered.

Charles' glare was heated and Darcy wondered if he had saved all of his anger for his sisters. Without another word, he pulled his jacket from the back of a chair and shrugged into it.

"Where are you going?" Caroline demanded. "You must be here if another gentleman comes to the door begging for you to meet his daughters—"

But Charles did not answer her, and strode from the room without a backward glance.

"He is being very difficult," Louisa said. "He should have forgotten the Bennet girl by now. It has been long enough, surely she has forgotten him."

Darcy tugged at his vest and reached for his own jacket. If Charles was heading in the direction Darcy supposed, he would do very well to follow.

"And now you will abandon us, too?" Caroline cried as Darcy pulled on his jacket.

"Indeed I shall be," Darcy said quickly. He kissed Georgiana's cheek and followed his friend out of the parlor.

Charles was halfway down the corridor by the time Darcy caught up with him.

"And where will you go?" he asked, already knowing the answer.

"To Longbourn," Charles replied. "I have unfinished business there."

Darcy kept pace with him, and his heart pounded in his chest as he realized how close he might be to his goal. "And so, Mr. Bennet was amenable to your suit?"

"He was, indeed. Most agreeable."

"And the young lady?"

"As her father expressed to me, it is entirely up to her. So, my hope rests on a very delicate thread," he said grimly.

Darcy nodded and they walked to the stables in silence. Darcy's mind churned with possibilities and the hope that Elizabeth would honor her word.

His duty was done, but he could not leave his friend to take the final step alone.

8

DARCY

The ride to Longbourn was only a few miles, a short jaunt on horseback, and Darcy's eagerness to reach their destination kept him from noticing the cold air that whipped at his cheeks.

Longbourn was not a large house, nor was it finely appointed or situated, but the grounds were pleasing, and the gardens were well maintained and had been planned by a careful eye with a mind to detail and function as well as beauty.

They would be quite something in the summer, of that he had no doubt.

Mr. Bingley dismounted as a young man ran from behind the house to take the reins of their horses. Darcy followed suit and threw his own reins at the startled young man before catching up with Charles who was already standing upon the front doorstep with his hand poised at the large wrought iron knocker.

"Are you certain?" Darcy asked quietly.

"More certain than I have ever been in all my life," Charles replied.

He looked at Darcy briefly, but Darcy could see that his friend was not looking for his approval. All he could do was smile.

"Go to it, man," he murmured.

Charles smiled and took hold of the knocker.

His strikes echoed in the foyer of the house and Charles stood back as the face of the Bennet's housekeeper appeared in the window, and then the door was pulled open.

He stood back to allow Charles to make his request to see the gentleman of the house, and turned to watch the young man that had come out to meet them as he led the horses around the side of the house—presumably to the stables where the horse that Jane Bennet had ridden to Netherfield Park in similar weather to this was kept.

Darcy was just about to turn back to his friend and accompany him into the house when a surprised voice caught him off his guard.

"Mr. Darcy?"

A pair of fine eyes, dark and expressive and widened in abject surprise, were the first thing he saw as Miss Elizabeth Bennet and a younger girl, presumably another Bennet sister, approached from the direction of the main road that led into Meryton.

He smiled briefly and then bowed as they came closer. "Miss Elizabeth Bennet," he greeted her. "A fine day for a walk, is it not?"

"It most certainly is not," said the younger girl. She pulled the spectacles from her face and wiped at the lenses crossly with the edge of her shawl.

"Go inside, Mary," Elizabeth whispered sternly. The girl nodded and without a word she walked past him at a brisk pace.

Charles Bingley had disappeared from the doorstep and Darcy breathed a small sigh of relief—

His duty was done, but he did not know if Elizabeth Bennet would agree.

Elizabeth smiled somewhat shakily up at him and Darcy felt some of his resolve weaken just a little.

"I am surprised to see you here," she said.

"Indeed," he replied. "I am surprised, myself, but I can only beg your forgiveness for the amount of time that has passed since we last spoke…"

"Several weeks," Elizabeth said.

"Indeed." Now he was repeating himself. "I have come here with Mr. Bingley," he blurted out.

"Yes, there has been some talk about town that Netherfield Park was occupied once more," Elizabeth said. "But I could not discern who precisely it was that had taken up residence. Our neighbors have not been as forthcoming as one would like."

Considering how Mr. Bingley and his party, himself included, had departed Netherfield Park; he could well understand the reluctance of the Bennet's neighbors to speak of something that could only cause pain.

"I hope you will accept my apologies," Darcy said. "I did not—"

Elizabeth shook her head. "An apology is not necessary," she said quietly. "I did not tell Jane that I had seen you in London. Nor did I tell her of the promise that you made… I could not see her heart broken any more than it already was." Her gaze flickered toward the house and she pulled her shawl tighter around her shoulders. "If Mr. Bingley and his sisters have returned to Netherfield Park that is their own business."

"But Miss Bennet— Elizabeth…" Darcy felt the desperate pounding of his heart in his chest and heard it in his ears. She could not misconstrue this… not after so much time had passed. "Mr. Bingley is here of his own accord."

"And I wish him joy of his time in Hertfordshire," Elizabeth replied. He could see the tension in her shoulders. She had not yet asked why he was here at Longbourn, and he could sense that she was afraid of what the answer might mean.

"There will be no joy in his stay here if he does not receive a favorable answer to a very important question." Darcy waited for his words to sink in, and did his best not to smile as the realization dawned upon Elizabeth's face.

"Mr. Bingley—is *here*..." she murmured.

"He is, indeed," Darcy said. "He spoke with your father upon our arrival—we came upon him in Meryton."

"But Mr. Bingley's sisters... Caroline and Louisa... They were both so vehemently opposed to the match— How—"

"Mr. Bingley has made the very important decision that he does not require their permission, or approval, when it comes to the matter of his personal affairs," Darcy replied.

It was true. Charles had become a changed man in a very short amount of time. Discovering the truth of his sister's opinions and prejudices against Jane Bennet had lit something aflame inside the usually amiable Mr. Bingley.

Though he would tell no one, Darcy was secretly thrilled to see his friend show some passion in obtaining what he truly desired in life.

Now, all that remained was to do the same for himself.

"Oh, Jane..." Elizabeth whispered and then looked up at him with tears in her dark eyes. "*You* have done this— you have done as you promised."

"I have," he replied.

He was taken by surprise again as Elizabeth rose up onto her toes and kissed him, very gently, and briefly at the corner of his mouth.

It took every bit of control to keep from pulling her into his arms and crushing her against his chest. He had thought about this moment for months. Perhaps even more than a year... But now that it was finally upon him, he knew that he had to be patient.

"I must speak to Jane," Elizabeth said breathlessly. "I will— I will send a letter..."

"I have brought my sister to Netherfield Park," Darcy said as she turned to leave. He reached out and grasped her hand gently. "I should very much like for you to meet her."

Elizabeth's shoulders dropped and she smiled warmly. Her fingers tightened on his briefly as she did so and Darcy's stomach twisted.

"I will meet her, of course," Elizabeth said and Darcy wondered if she knew how important such a meeting was. Surely, it could not have escaped her notice.

She had sisters herself, and their opinion was no doubt important to her.

"I must go to Jane," Elizabeth continued. "Thank you…"

Darcy released her hand and bowed. "I gave you my word, as a gentleman."

"Indeed, and you have kept it," Elizabeth said breathlessly before she turned and ran back through the courtyard to the house.

Alone in front of the house, Darcy did not know what to do with himself, but before he could begin to pace the gravel, Mr. Bingley appeared in the doorway.

"Come inside, man," his friend said with a grin. "We have been commanded to stay for tea."

Darcy felt that same hope flare in his chest as Jane Bennet appeared at Charles' side. "Yes, Mr. Darcy, do come in. It looks like it shall rain again," she said with a smile.

Darcy hurried to comply, surprised at his own eagerness to partake in such a mundane affair. But perhaps this would give him a chance to pursue his own suit… if he could feel half of the happiness his friend exuded he knew that he would be the happiest of men when his own time came.

The rumors that Georgiana had spoken of were, indeed, true. An assembly had been planned, though it was not clear whether or not Charles was behind it. He would neither confirm nor deny their accusations, and though Caroline and Louisa complained bitterly, they could not escape.

Charles' proposal to Jane Bennet had been very well received, and as his sisters adjusted to the idea of their brother's marriage the tension in the house had begun to subside. It had not disappeared, but it had lessened and Darcy was grateful for it.

Jane Bennet, joined most often by Elizabeth, came to tea regularly at Netherfield Park, and she seemed willing to forget and forgive the egregious slights that Mr. Bingley's sisters had paid to her after their departure from Netherfield Park. In fact, it was not spoken of at all.

As Darcy had hoped, Georgiana and Elizabeth seemed very well suited as friends, and Darcy hoped that such affection as he witnessed between them would only strengthen when Elizabeth agreed to be his wife.

But therein was the problem. He had not had occasion to ask her.

He had spoken to her father and obtained his permission to present his suit—but Elizabeth had already refused him once before, and that memory still stung him in the most uncomfortable of ways.

Her refusal had been his fault, of that he was very much aware.

He chose to keep his distance during their visits and preferred, instead, to watch Elizabeth's interactions with Georgiana and listen to their lively conversations.

If he had not thought that his admiration for this young woman could grow in such a short time, he had been very much mistaken. Georgiana seemed very taken with Elizabeth as well, and Darcy knew that she would support their union whole-heartedly.

"But you must come here to prepare for the assembly," Georgiana cried. "Please, say that you will, then we shall arrive together."

The assembly, and Christmas, were only days away, and the excitement in the house was palpable. On the occasions that they were invited to Longbourn, it was impossible to deny that something wonderful was about to happen.

Darcy looked up from the letter he was writing to meet Elizabeth's brief glance and then looked away as her cheeks flushed slightly.

"I do not see why we could not," Jane said with a smile. "We shall all arrive together."

Georgiana clapped her hands gaily. She was accustomed to having her wishes granted in short order, and Jane seemed eager to comply.

A house full of women, he thought.

But perhaps it would also afford him the opportunity he needed to speak to Elizabeth… to ask her—nay—to beg her to be his wife.

9

ELIZABETH

Kitty had been sorely disappointed that she had not been invited to come to Netherfield Park to prepare for the assembly, but her complaints were hushed by Mrs. Bennet who seemed more than eager to have her eldest daughters spend as much time as possible at Netherfield Park.

Elizabeth noticed that she seemed especially concerned about Elizabeth's closeness to Georgiana Darcy, and could only assume that her mother's interest had everything to do with a proposal from the gentleman who loomed at the edge of their every interaction.

She was well aware that she had kept him waiting. He had kept his promise—it was now she who was holding all of the proverbial cards.

If she truly wished it, she could reject him yet again.

But it would have been easy enough for him to lie—easy enough to pretend that his promise did not matter. But he had brought Mr. Bingley back to Hertfordshire, and Jane—dear Jane had never been happier.

They were to be married in the new year, and Elizabeth could hardly keep her joy at bay to see her elder sister glowing with the love she held for the smiling gentleman from London.

They had thought never to see the Bingleys again, but now the lights were lit at Netherfield Park, and there had been no talk of when they might return to London.

But Elizabeth had lain awake for far too many nights while she had pondered what she might do. All of her pondering, however, had hinged on her belief that the gentleman would do nothing—his sudden presence at Longbourn, and Mr. Bingley's unexpected proposal, had taken her completely by surprise.

Certainly, some part of her had hoped that this might happen. But to have it become a reality instead of a fevered wish—she did not know how to approach it, or how to manage the rush of emotion that threatened to sweep her away at any given moment.

On the day of the assembly, a carriage arrived from Netherfield Park to carry them, and all of their boxes and valises, away from Longbourn. Kitty's pout was heart wrenching, but their mother would not be convinced that she should also be able to prepare for the evening away from Longbourn.

Elizabeth did her best not to notice the way that Mr. Darcy and Mr. Bingley hovered at the edge of their activities and tried, instead, to focus on the pleasure of preparing for the evening's festivities without the usual chaos of Longbourn spinning around them.

The drama and excitement of their house had lessened somewhat since Lydia's departure, but Kitty had put a good deal of effort into filling the space that Lydia had vacated, both in noise and in dramatics.

It was a relief to be away from her, at least for one evening. Elizabeth knew very well that she would spend a good amount of time making certain that Kitty did not make an embarrassment of herself during the assembly as she danced with every officer who looked in her direction.

It was a thought she did not have often, but perhaps Lydia's marriage had been a blessing in disguise. For Kitty's sake, if nothing else.

As the hour of their departure drew closer, Elizabeth found herself thinking of Mr. Darcy more often. She knew that he was watching their preparations, or at the very least, listening from the drawing room, and her desire to speak to him began to grow to an overwhelming desire.

She had put it off long enough.

Elizabeth was dressed, a pale pink confection of a gown that was, for once, not something she had borrowed from Jane's wardrobe. The sleeves and hems were edged with dark rose ribbon, and a length of black velvet ribbon, studded with roses made from the same ribbon that hemmed her gown had been fixed into her hair. She felt beautiful, and Georgiana had confirmed it breathlessly as she had slid the final hairpin into Elizabeth's dark curls.

She made her apologies and excused herself from the parlor where Louisa was putting the final touches on Jane's hairstyle and stepped out into the corridor. Elizabeth was not certain what she might say to Mr. Darcy, all she knew was that she owed the gentleman her gratitude—if he were to be bold enough to remind her of her own promise, perhaps he would be rewarded with her answer.

But Mr. Darcy was not in the drawing room, nor the library... Elizabeth walked down the corridor, confused, she did not wish to run through the house calling out his name... but it seemed as though that would be her only option.

As she walked into the foyer, she noticed a flash of movement in the courtyard.

Finally.

With her heart pounding in her chest, Elizabeth pulled open the front door and stepped out into the chilled evening air. The sunset had painted the gathering clouds in tones of pink and orange and she took a quick breath at the sharpness of the wind as it swept over her bare arms. She thought briefly that she should have brought a shawl, but it was too late now.

"Miss Bennet? You should not be out here—"

Mr. Darcy came around to the front of the house and Elizabeth could not help the smile that spread over her face.

"I came to find you," she said in a rush. "But you were not in the drawing room—"

"I have been speaking to the carriage driver," he said. "All is in readiness for our departure to the assembly rooms…"

"Wonderful," she said and then felt foolish for saying so.

"Was there something you needed?"

His dark eyes held hers captive and Elizabeth bit down on her lip to remind herself of why she had gone in search of him.

"I— That is… I wanted to thank you," she said haltingly.

He stepped closer, blocking the wind with his body and Elizabeth smiled up at him.

"For what?"

"For what you have done for Jane," Elizabeth said. "If you had not— I do not know what might have happened to her. I suspect that she would have wasted her life here in Hertfordshire, unhappy and alone."

"And you?" he asked. "What would you have done?"

"Me?"

Elizabeth was startled by his gentle question. She had not given any thought to what her life might have been like if he had not followed through on his promise. Perhaps she would have moved on… but could she have trusted any gentleman again?

"I do not know," she replied honestly.

His hands captured hers and Elizabeth shivered at the sudden warmth that enveloped them.

"And now that your sister is to be wed? Are you happy?"

"I am," Elizabeth said firmly. She looked at their clasped hands and could not ignore the desperate pounding of her heart against her ribs.

"There was more than one promise made in London," he murmured.

He had done it.

Her smile faltered, but then she found her own boldness.

"There was," she replied. "And you have fulfilled your promise and brought with it all of Jane's hopes and dreams."

"But what of your own hopes and dreams?"

"Mine…"

"If you say that you do not wish to see me again, I shall leave Hertfordshire tonight and you shall hear from me no more," he said.

The thought of him leaving pierced Elizabeth's chest like the point of a knife.

"No," she choked out. "I would have you stay."

"Would you?"

She nodded vigorously.

"Why would you wish for that?"

"Because—"

Why could she not say it? Why could she not say the words that clamored on the tip of her tongue and etched themselves upon her heart?

"Because I love you," she choked out. "Most ardently…"

His dark gaze held her captive, and she wished that he would kiss her so that she would not have to speak any more. Words were confusing, and troublesome, and she wished to be silent. What if he rejected her? What if he had decided that she was too much trouble for any man to spend a life with—

"Will you be my wife?" he asked simply.

"Yes," she whispered. "I will."

Elizabeth closed her eyes as his lips met hers. The kiss was gentle, but there was a heat of promise behind it that could not be denied. She wanted nothing more than to be crushed against his chest, but Mr. Darcy's fingers held hers softly and when he pulled away, it was with great reluctance.

Elizabeth opened her eyes, but she did not want the moment to end.

"We must be married at once," he said. "I cannot bear the thought of waiting to call you Mrs. Darcy."

Tears threatened to spill over her cheeks, and Elizabeth laughed softly as she pulled her hand away from his to wipe at the errant tears that prickled at her lashes. As she looked out over the gently rolling hills that surrounded Netherfield Park, her breath caught in her throat as she realized that the chill in the air had grown sharper and she pressed against Darcy's chest.

"Snow," she murmured as the first flakes began to fall. They landed on her bare shoulder and she shivered before wiping it away with the tip of her finger. "Just in time for Christmas."

"Just in time for us," he said as he touched her chin gently to tilt her head up for another kiss. As Elizabeth melted against him, it seemed impossible that she had denied herself a chance at happiness for so long. But any sacrifice would have been worth it to see Jane happy.

But fate had been kind, and now she and her sister could both celebrate the unexpected, and hard won, love that had swept them away.

THE END